THE B

THE BOOK OF
STYXHEXENHAMMER

HOW I HATE SOCIETY AND LIKE SPOONS

Tarl Warwick
2018

1

COPYRIGHT AND DISCLAIMER

FOREWORD

LOL

CONTENTS

THE BOOK OF STYXHEXENHAMMER

INTRODUCTION

One of the greatest curses of being a workaholic perfectionist is that you get trapped in a never ending cycle of repeatedly trying to build, improve, and compete. It can be addictive- it's not really the opposite of being lazy and a deadbeat, it's really just a form of more generally socially tolerated addiction just like sitting on the couch eating potato chips and burping is.

For those of us, then, that seek to always expand our reach and put down our various foes, what can be done for leisure? I am, by career, an author, editor, political analyst, and garden hobbyist- quite a slew of work to do, since I want to slowly rise up through the ranks of all of these things- the garden has to expand, the soil be more and more built, the videos won't just make themselves, and every time I see a crappy self published title on the internet where someone slapped an age-old pdf into a file and called it complete it makes me foam with rage and I get the urge to edit it myself more meticulously. How then shall I relax for a bit when I can't relax when not being productive?

It came to me; why not write a humorous manuscript, sort of an inside joke for people that are already patrons of my work? Hell, maybe someone unfamiliar with me will read this and get a chuckle, or scratch their head and say "what am I doing with my life, reading this?" Actually the latter is more my kind of humor anyways. I was "that kid" in school that would purposely tell shitty jokes in order to get a negative reaction because the inevitable point was to confuse or dismay the listener, so that I could roar with insane laughter (and I did. I was an odd child.)

THE BOOK OF STYXHEXENHAMMER

Some people enjoy poetry, some enjoy prose. Mine usually revolves around bodily functions unless it deals with folklore, spirituality, or politics.

Here then is a semirandom compilation of material without any real purpose that you may or may not enjoy. If you do, that's good and I am glad. If not, oh well, that's ok too- everyone has things they don't enjoy. I don't enjoy quiche, or shepherds' pie recipes that call for carrots or peas. I also don't enjoy the burning sensation of being bitten by a spider that was too stupid not to crawl into my shoe thinking all the while to itself "heehee nobody is living in this mansion yet."

Is there really a plot, or any deal of significant organization to this work? No. Is it of great critical importance likely to win awards? Hell no, but when the nobel prize can go to someone who subsequently slaughters tens of thousands of civilians using flying robots we should probably ask ourselves if awards mean literally anything at all. I have a silver (plated) play button from Youtube and a bronze plaque on my wall from Bitchute- those are probably more meaningful these days than a nobel prize, and certainly more so than any prize awarded to "journalists" or news sites.

So sit back and leer at this volume by dim candle light while stroking your deformed, vivisected pet chimera, or maybe act like a normal person and enjoy reading this lunacy anyways.

I: TELLING THE FUTURE BY SPOONS FOR NO REASON

Sit ye, listen and behold a method by which thou mayest tell the future.

You must gather a number of spoons between five and eleven, but the number must be odd. You must place said spoons in a vessel such that when shaken the spoons may freely move. Sit upon the floor and ask a question of the spoon gods- it must be able to be answered in the form of yes or no. Cast the spoons before you from the vessel, and observe them. If the number of spoons facing you (that is, the large end of the spoon is closer than the handle) is greater than the number facing away, you may be sure that the answer is affirmative. If not, the spoon gods answer "no."

Once an answer has been made, there is no doing the question again to get a different result, and may result in angry cutlery. If the question is time sensitive (for example, "should I go for a hike today?") then after that time has elapsed a similar question may again be made.

These spoons should be consecrated before usage by incensing them. Place, in their vessel, a cone of white sage incense and allow the smoke to flow. If the vessel is not safe to incense in this way, you may burn the incense next to it instead but it is better that the vessel be steel or clay and thus impermeable to fire.

II: MAKING VIDEOS IS COOL

I just thought I should expound in some degree of detail some of the cool things about making videos on the internet- I can remember some young adult "spooky" show back in the late 90s- I think it was called "So Weird"- where the protagonist had a website and posted weird shit about the paranormal. The idea at the time seemed like space age stuff- now everyone and their mother has an online presence and toddlers can use a smartphone more easily than I can (I never owned one because they're a government tracking and wrongthink monitoring spy gadget that was foisted on people in the name of convenience that just makes them a bunch of frenetic gerbils incapable of functioning autonomously. It's a microcosm of authoritarianism- a slave device, a collar of sorts for a perverted people.)

The first really cool aspect is the mere thought that somewhere in Nepal or maybe Chile someone is watching your content. It's surreal to think of, that someone who barely speaks your language might be watching you anyways solely because someone they in turn enjoy posted your content, or because you're covering an event they have interest in.

Second to this- and this is no lie- it's pretty damn funny to think of someone half a world away potentially becoming physically attracted to you for one reason or another. Sometimes this isn't even quite fair- the camera can hide blemishes and we artificially limit what the public sees when we make such content, thus stripping elements of our actual existence (personality etc) out and providing what amounts to a sanitized self view. It's funny how this affects the creator perhaps more than the absorber of their content- over time they may develop a false self awareness that has been influenced by others- they stare into the abyss and are changed by it, so to speak.

8

THE BOOK OF STYXHEXENHAMMER

Nonetheless it is amusing to make content- it doesn't have to solely be video; it thrills me to think of someone holding a copy of this book and reading it, maybe in between college courses or as a late night pre-bed ritual. That pleases me, and books are superior to video in the sense of both aesthetics and mental ease; not as involved, more relaxing overall, although there's some ASMR I've seen that really works to ease insomnia a bit.

I was already making (primitive 360p) videos in 2007. It was a major milestone when Youtube developed 720 capabilities and a 15 minute limit to replace the older 10 minute one. Even better was when buffering no longer took five minutes for a minute long video. Now it isn't just their site- Bitchute, Steemit, and many others are proliferating, although some of those sites will eventually collapse just as many did years ago when people first began to look for a new hosting site in the wake of what was termed the "adpocalypse." My first video on Youtube was called "ghost" and was basically just me playing with webcam filters and trying to figure out how to make objects semitransparent. My second video was a darkly psychedelic video combining various effects over which played Depeche Mode's "Nothing's Impossible." I can't remember the other first few I made but the only one early on which got any real attention was a mashup of Talk Talk's "Life's What You Make It" and some footage from Pink Floyd's "The Wall" with Empty Spaces playing. Just a slight bit of Styxhexenhammer origin story. By the way I almost didn't become Styxhexenhammer; my ICQ username at the time was JohnLennon and I almost made some permutation of his name mine for the platform.

III: MY ENEMIES ARE DUMB

They say the easiest person to rob is a thief because they are never expecting to be robbed. Likewise, the censorious enemies that have tried to cling onto me like ticks to a squirrel are hilariously setting themselves up to be suppressed in due course. I've thought for some time now, that it's odd that whenever these people are abused, they come to people like me to help them; this isn't a partisan thing- the earliest attempts I ever faced as a creator on any platform, to censor and destroy my content, were on Facebook and mostly involved hyper-religious and usually right wing evangelicals attempting to attack my anti-Dubya Bush content and my anti-war pages. Fairly soon thereafter the same usual crowd of far right and religious people attacked me on Youtube. Much like the far left as of the time of writing this, they always used the excuse of wanting to deplatform hate filled or degenerated individuals for some reason; it was a social panic then and it is one now as well.

When I look back at the mid 2000s I laugh because people like me who stood up against the lamestream then are now regarded as having done what was right- but at the time it was largely regarded as "treason" or "being a malcontent" or something of that type. Nowadays, if you resist censorship and the malevolence of big government and corporations, you're a "nazi" or something. I've seen some goofy people even try to claim that people who have never said anything hateful are "gateway drugs" to neonazism because they dare to criticize the establishment. If these people weren't almost horrendously mentally bereft they'd be able to be easily shown that what they're saying is nothing more than an amusing doppelganger of what George W Bushes' war happy fans said fifteen years prior.

There have been quite a few times where I've considered,

for a time, the possibility of sitting the next moral panic out, staying on the sidelines and not getting involved; I'm well aware of the fact that my life would be substantially easier and my income probably higher if I just went with the flow, and joined the mainstream, which after all is nothing more than a river of stale urine filled with foulness, but a conscience is a terrible thing (even if helpful or noble) and won't let me.

It's funny to watch the opportunists gathering around the book-fueled bonfire of moralism. Like the idiots of past eras- the moralists of the temperance movement, the McCarthyists, the anti-Harry Potter crowd of the 90s, they will inevitably collapse as a movement. If you should stand in the dark and light a torch, it won't be long before moths are attracted to it- it also won't be long til there are some roasted dead moths at your feet because they get close, thinking the torch is sunlight, or something, and then the wind changes and flashes their wings clean off in a wave of fire. I have sympathy for the moths because they are just insects and cannot be counted on to do much that doesn't involve brutish instinct- I do not have sympathy for most humans who engage in similar behavior because they should know better.

All they need to do is study the last century or so of US history alone and they can observe a half dozen major social panics- Temperance, McCarthyism, the space race (subjugated to the atomic arms race partly), the Satanic Panic, 9/11 (and the war on terror in part), and the current internet based moralism in which the far right and far left both seek to make everyone miserable.

In my own opinion anyone who endorses deplatforming is a fool even if they do so for vengeful reasons; perhaps especially if they do so because it shows they comprehend the unjust nature of the act aimed at its progenitor victims in the first place. I see primarily people who consider themselves to be "conservative" or something similar engaging in this because it is mostly those who proclaim themselves "liberal" or "progressive" who are primordially attempting to give corporations limitless censorship abilities; literally, liberals so-called are attempting to hand over the world on a silver platter to a bunch of businesses whose wealth makes the rail and steel and coal barons of the late 1800s gilded age seem like nothing more than slightly interesting serfs. Businesses which outsource crappy jobs to India or Thailand or buy computer components from China where they are made by child slaves using raw minerals mined by North Korean peasant laborers.

In truth these terms are meaningless; there is no such thing as a "liberal" or a "conservative"- these terms only exist in the confused minds of their own self-adhering users; but the liberal self-described is little more than a fascist who has been convinced that the violent activities of fascism are acceptable and virtuous so long as they are aimed at self-described "conservatives" and the opposite is also true. Even libertarianism barely exists as it has been propagandistically warped beyond its original form into an odd sort of anarcho-communism in which globalist open borders are strangely applauded as being compatible with a limited government culture of constitution-worship.

Those few of us not totally subsumed by newspeak and propaganda are in a bind; we want liberty (because we are not dumb and understand the issues of totalitarianism) but cannot actually prevent authoritarianism without ourselves using authoritarian tactics to break through layers of linguistic mind-melting propaganda. The propaganda is so thick and prevalent and common that the only way to wake a person up is to deploy counterpropaganda; which of course anyone with a bit of intellect can determine is, itself, just propaganda as well of a sort, if benevolent.

THE BOOK OF STYXHEXENHAMMER

Our enemies are in a similar bind after a sort of fashion; they want to defend civilization by destroying it completely because they have been convinced that philosophies, laws, and cultural trappings which are innately and obviously harmful are to be applauded, lest the culture be "hateful." It escapes the notice of these smaller, supposedly progressive minds that in so adopting such means they are actually hating their own culture- one which will ultimately and inevitably die along with its progress so-called and its tolerance because stronger individuals will supplant it. While we might hope those new masters are kind and benevolent classical liberals they're more likely to be tyrannical communists or national socialists or perhaps theocratic in nature and will grind the population down into despotic worthlessness.

This is what I fight against. It's a thankless and life-long battle because each successive moral panic recedes only to eventually give way to another. In a perfect world thus the enemies of creators, of those who believe in being left alone and limiting the corrupting powers that be, would not exist and people would be less troubled- but mankind is like a crustacean on the rocky shores of a foamy sea- now battered by waves, and then dehydrated by the hot sun. He has to take cover, slide into the murky slime of a tidal pool just to survive- a bizarre and phantasmagorical world of contradictory cultural values and opportunists always seeking, like a barracuda preying upon that selfsame crustacean- to destroy the entirety of all that is good and dignified about the human race.

IV: LYKE SO TOTALLY RANDOM D00D

And now we must dispense a few factoids.

-I am morbidly enraged by dudes who have this one weird body type that is thankfully not common; it's a little like dwarfism but it isn't- they're of normal or near normal height and have arms that are just slightly too short for their body, and usually a bit more density in the chest area than looks normal; not muscular per se, indeed every time I see a dude like this he looks chubby, just bulky, after a fashion. Mark Zuckerberg looks kind of like this, although recently it looks like he lost ten pounds for no reason so maybe they just removed a couple of his android implants or something.

-The concept of insanity is one of the funniest things to me. I saw an episode of "Gunsmoke" once (my grandfather used to watch it every single day, sometimes ten show marathons) and at the end of the episode, some generic "bad guy" that Matt Dillon had hauled in was in the upper floor of a hotel, under house arrest I think, and went absolutely bonkers and started laughing like a maniac while wheeling around with a bottle of what had to be whiskey. As the townspeople below looked on awestruck, he told them something to the effect that he was better than them because he took whatever he wanted. Then he fell down and died. I thought this was hilarious. As a smaller child I always liked the show "Winnie the Pooh" because Tigger would occasionally go spastic for a while. I always thought the rabbit should have smacked him in the neck a couple of times to calm his ass down.

-Sometimes people have speculated that I make videos (sometimes or always) while not wearing any pants, because they only ever see me, mostly, from the midriff up. This is actually totally untrue and I have only ever made videos while fully clothed. Conversely, I used to troll ICQ chat while totally naked because of aforementioned glee at insanity- including pretending to be insane. I would sit and laugh like a hyena until the back of my throat hurt while slowly demoralizing the moderation staff and causing people to lose faith in humanity.

-Some people don't realize it but my book "Sickness In Hell", while definitively only for the 18+ audience, began to take form before I was 18 years of age and is a very loose adaptation of the first third or so of a horror work I began when I was literally still in the ninth grade. I wasn't even old enough to get a copy of Grand Theft Auto on my own and I had written a (meandering but good-for-my-age) novella of sorts where a middle management consultant goes insane and starts hallucinating about a seven foot tall cowboy that encourages him to become a mass murderer, after which he guts a pregnant woman, dehydrates the fetus, and eats it with a bag of dried apricots. I became directionless and abandoned the project around the time I wrote myself into a corner where he would have had to gain supernatural aid to have escaped being killed around page 120 or so as a whole legion of police managed to surround him after he used a makeshift flamethrower to burn several city blocks to the ground, shooting and killing fleeing civilians.

-The brook outside my home in Rutland routinely spawns extremely nice pieces of driftwood suitable for use as staffs. I had one shaped a bit like the grim reapers' blade years ago but it got lost somehow. Now I have one that looks vaguely like a Gandalf stick.

-I have a small collection of vintage 1980s era cologne and a massive collection of vintage 1980s era bamboo wall scrolls which were popular during the Asian invasion of modern art at the time. It's probably the only good modern art other than modernist art deco since it's a style technically most popular in the wake of American GI forces returning from the occupation of Japan after World War Two with various portraits and pictures printed on silk.

-Flowers from my garden are growing in a number of other states because I have sent seeds to other people on occasion. I swear that I never sent any that were prohibited due to invasive status but I did get briefly investigated by the Vermont Department of Agriculture once because I bought corn seeds from China not realizing that it is illegal to plant most species of seeds if they came from foreign nations through private channels (I never planted them because I had run out of room so I didn't get fined or anything but it was still hilarious.)

-When I was a little kid, I wasn't into gothic or hippie styles like I am today and actually preferred flannel shirts and cowboy hats. The closest thing I ever wore to my modern outfits was a black denim coat I had for a while when I was maybe seven or so.

-Shepherds' pie is one of the tastiest foods. I eat it with ketchup like I do macaroni and cheese, burgers, hot dogs, fries, tater tots, and much more- but one time when I was young, my mother added sour cream to it thinking "hey, sour cream goes with potato and potato is in shepherds' pie"- needless to say it was the one time I did not clean my plate and immediately desire that ketchupy plate of seconds. Also I have no idea why some people add carrots or peas to shepherds' pie- it should be made with herby, buttery mashed potato in a layer separating a nice thick layer of corn and a slightly crisped layer of seasoned hamburger. Nothing else.

V: SPIDER CIDER

There's an interesting idea I thought of years ago when I was writing a short joke manuscript based on the band "Enbilulugugal" called spider cider. This substance is basically nothing more than a large number of spiders, liquefied into the proper base liquid, much like you may use tomato or perhaps cucumber juices as a base for some sort of supposedly cleansing but ultimately half-useless vegetable juice purge.

The first step of this wonderful concept is to generate swarms of prey for the spiders you will need. Breeding spiders is hard but allowing them to replicate under conditions in which their food supply is more or less to be considered limitless is simple. In my booklet on the infamous goat-loving noise band, I suggested this could be done easily if a person did little more than leave a pile of composting matter in the middle of a basement or something like that. This pile, which should be a hundred pounds of fermenting matter or more, will generate a literal legion of flies in mere weeks, so assuming the home you are in (or outbuilding!) is well built most of those flies will be around inside, buzzing and humping each other like insects tend to do, and will largely be incapable of escaping.

Once this has happened, the natural reaction follows; spiders (and other predatory bugs) will infest the area and slowly begin to whittle away at the fly population. So long as new composted manure or rotten fruity matter is added the flies will continue to swarm and the predators will replicate endlessly. Vegetable matter is ok but less effective while meat will tend to make the area uninhabitable due to being too smelly. I recommend fruit and manure.

After some months of sly swarms, composting cow

manure, and spider replication, the grand feast is not likely to be far ahead. Spider webs look slightly like cotton candy (although they do not have a flavor) and so a simple method may be used to gather what will become the epic spider cider- take a couple sticks and gather some webs until they form a net- now dash around haphazardly gathering flies up, occasionally also grabbing more webs on the sticks and the spiders along with them, which will be trapped between each webby layer.

This insect-ridden mass of cotton-candy style webs will eventually be considerable in size. It is now merely a matter of infusing the drippings from its captive spider population into some other liquid.

The simplest solution is to drown the spiders in your liquid. You could even pickle them with vinegar, salt, and dill and make spidery pickles, which would be an extra spooky Samhain treat, but for easier access to this grand food item it is possible to simply press the gathered webs in a vice between two sheets of metal and let the liquefied spider and fly guts drip out into whatever liquid is considered desirable. Bon apetit!

VI: I AM SO GREAT

And now gather around as I tell you the super important tale of my time on ICQ chat where, like a masked and unidentifiable bandit, I existed not as "Styxhexenhammer" but as "JohnLennon." I have related this tale in part in video form but I used to have a much more elaborate origin story back before the recent crackdown on all interesting online content. Rather than hazard all my other work I deleted the blog that had once held hundreds of hysterical and amazing posts made during the course of two years' time spent at war with the Ops on ICQ chat.

Why, you may ask, would I be great for having trolled some secondary website years ago? Why, for the glory of liberation of course. ICQ chat no longer exists- at least the one run by the people who were there at the time, some of them have their own chat sites now (which range from empty to nearly empty) and the rest I guess gave up and decided to modernize and get with the 2010s.

When I first arrived on ICQ chat I was not well known- indeed I started using their service before I even had a Youtube channel- for a couple months there I was pretty much known as an anti-war Facebook user and militant atheist (later Satanist) on their chatting site, which at the time was not only large but absolutely massive; there had to be some tens of thousands of active users at all hours when I first arrived, and it wasn't until well into the 2010s that their site was nonfunctionally empty and no longer amusing for anything but trolling.

Anyways, my first time connecting there was through a (still extant) website called "Wicca Chat" because I wanted to discuss religion with them and learn more about their interesting mannerisms and beliefs. It wasn't long before I discovered that the service was larger than just this one site page and included other chatrooms full of pagans, gamers, political junkies, and even vampires self-professed. Fairly quickly I realized there was also a room full of christians which was funny since I liked debating people.

Most of the rooms on the site were run by people who were reasonably fair and not quick to ban people but that was not the case on the christian room. At least one of the moderators who enjoyed harassing me and every other nonchristian is now dead so I won't mention names, but I quickly realized it was hysterically fun to bait them into debates, after which they almost always antagonized both myself and other users- this led to chaos and usually multiple suspensions. For about a year I only did this sporadically and because of college work ended up abandoning chatrooms for the better part of a year or so (I think it was 2008 or '09. By the time I came back ICQ had fewer people and the moderators had changed quite a bit and not always for the better.

I eventually realized it was a duty of mine as a newly minted liberty loving real liberal (libertarian) to defend against tyranny. It wasn't that I cared what rules were imposed, but the moderators were ignoring them and banning even those who objectively did nothing wrong, sometimes even banning their usernames. I began a severe campaign to grind the moderators down in the christianity chatroom and over several months ICQ slowly became a haven for people who were literally only there to stir up debate or spam rooms. Eventually the moderators of not just the christian room but several others had their rooms delisted, causing them to collapse as new users could never even find them. Since the religious rooms were quite popular before this blew a massive hole in the sites' daily user base and led to its quicker decline.

For another year or so things pretty much stayed the same; I went into the room three or four times a week, loaded them with trolls from other websites, and caused uproar, until it became so passe that some regular users just stopped using the site. Since I was doing this to punish moderators that never listened when I told them some of their coworkers were abusing people I ended up with a small fan club of sorts which found the attacks hilarious and supported my work. I even sang songs about my exploits, much to the glee of onlookers. Even the head moderator of the whole website decided to comment (negatively) on some of my video content although after the website collapsed entirely it seems she buried the hatchet so I leave her chat site alone.

Then, one strange day, all of a sudden all of the anti-spam bots were gone along with all the moderators' ability to moderate. They didn't want to discuss why, and I (correctly) surmised that big changes were ahead. After a day of chaos in which the site suffered from a severe slowdown and constant spam raids, their mod status was restored, but the damage was done and the site continued its decline. I declared that day to be "D Day" and began trolling them with my blog, saying we were in a world war and likening myself to General Patton overseeing some major operations into Fortress Europe.

It wasn't even a year before the moderators were purged altogether. Because of trolling and spam led by me personally the administrators of ICQ's parent company had decided to fire every site operator and all the moderators on every listed room-without them, and the bots they administered personally, the site became a hellhole of abuse and chaos and my forces reigned for many weeks, attacking rooms at a whim and breaking rules that no longer existed as one final victory lap before the website was closed down as unusable by its parent firm altogether. Lennonism, at long last, won.

The lessons I learned during this period have literally shaped parts of my professional life.

-I realized that authority figures were often out of touch with their fans, audience, subjects, etc, even when they were not nearly powerful enough to properly justify their apparent ignorance of peoples' concerns.

-I realized the intense value of free speech by recognizing how sad things truly were when even potentially disruptive activity was censored.

-I realized it was possible, through concerted long term effort, to subvert and destroy the abusive by various means.

-I realized that ICQ wasn't just a stand alone chatting service but was also a surprisingly profitable and popular messaging app, and continues to be to this day despite the loss of one of its main services used by a formerly decent-sized US audience.

Some people, at the time, thought my behavior was a waste of time and that it was holding me back. Not only do I disagree but I consider it one of the most important foundations of all of my current success.

VII

From when I was a kid in elementary school there are always some things that I remember more than others. Once this literature teacher told us a story that involved a pair of kids, one of who died, and wolves then disinterring the corpse the next day while the other kid was half asleep in a fever dream. I can't remember the rest of the story but I had nightmares for a while. There was another one where some crazy old witch was trying to kill these kids that were hiding up a tree and she was chanting a spell to cut it down while one of the children up above was using a counterspell to make it keep growing more trunk to stop her. I think the wicked witch got her throat torn out by the kids dog at the end.

Still again we went to a performance once (one of those shitty ones where one dude with a guitar rambles and all the theater and English teachers applaud marvelously) which was about a man who bought a magical bird but then eventually got bored with it or thought it was evil so he kept trying to get rid of it and it kept coming back- he tried tossing it in a box and into the river, chopping it in half and burying it, etc. I thought that was pretty morbid for a first grade class, and it was funny because one of my classmates kept replacing one of the lines of the story with flatulence humor. The best story though was this weird African folk tale (or at least it was presented to us as one) in which a Rhinocerous had somehow cheated another animal somehow (I think out of food) and ended up permanently screwed- apparently the rhino only has wrinkled skin because some other being convinced it to go bathe in the river and, while its skin was off, the other animal put bread crumbs inside, causing so much itching the skin got funky. Why the Rhino didn't skin the other animal and wear his flesh I am not sure.

VIII: I AM SLIGHTLY OBSESSED WITH 1980s ERA BAMBOO SCROLLS

Some of my fans may know this but I am kind of obsessed with a certain kind of retro-deco art form that was popular during the silk-and-bamboo days of the late 1970s through the early 1990s, peaking in around 1983 or so, in which extremely detailed works were printed on bamboo scrolls and often glued to backings or even to walls themselves (which ruins the back of the scroll so I never do so. I'd rather pinhole the wall with a tack to hang them.) These ornate scrolls come in multiple designs and some date further back, to the middle of the 1970s (there are 1976 bicentennial bamboo calendars that were made) but most of them are straight from the 1980s.

I bring this up because this may be the first time that the subject has ever actually been written about except coincidentally, such as a work of modern Asian art pieces perhaps mentioning the existence of such works. As far as I can tell they can be grouped into three distinct categories.

1. Authentic works from the mid 70s through the early 90s. They are printed on bamboo.

2. Modern remakes from the early 90s through the modern period which are often on balsam wood, not bamboo. (Balsam wood has a bit of a shine to it and is not as strong. These appear to be largely Chinese in manufacture.)

3. Works predating the mid 70s often on silk. They are authentic but not identical to the ones I have interest in.

It should be noted that similar scrolls made of plastic are

common today, as well as painted wood. The progenitor art form dates to the 1940s, stylistically, at least as a commodity in the west. Those works are on silk although some modern silk hangs are made also. Silk was popular in the 1980s as well so there are numerous works of the kind, often depicting the same three subjects; floral arrangements, women, or birds.

Due to a mark on one of the hangs I was able to judge that there are at a minimum roughly 400 different designs involved in those that are authentic in nature to the style I myself prefer to collect. Some of the more modern pieces are not hand painted (as almost all of the older ones are!) and can be told apart by several methods.

1. Print is on balsam, not bamboo.

2. Print lacks a signature, which should be in red ink.

3. Print depicts anything postmodern such as automobiles or western style homes instead of Asian diaspora subjects.

4. The piece is blurred, indicating it may have been printed by a machine and mass produced (this is not always the case. Since pieces were handmade, some may have blurred parts due to the stylistic inclination of the artist, or due to simple mistake that nonetheless did not preclude sale.)

I have great interest in and will continue to study this subject for some time and potentially produce a full work on it when I have amassed a larger collection. As of this moment, I have roughly 50 scrolls, including a few duplicates which I purchased for comparison purposes.

IX: THE TALE OF TURNIP-THULHU

Once in this last growing season I unearthed a turnip from my garden bigger around than a grapefruit and crenelated with horrific scars and pockmarks from being eaten away at by insects. Mostly, turnips have one main root system, but this one had several, probably due to deformity when it was still young.

This horrendous being was tormented and tortured during its time face-first in the dirt, its leeching tentacles plowing ever so slowly deeper and deeper into increasingly barren stratum. In the first few inches of soil were excellent nutrients, even below that for a few more, good tilth at least, but this abomination, ever masochistic, had worked its stringy arms deeper into blackness, presumably to avoid the light. Its leaves were filled with small holes- painful remnant evidence that it had been predated upon. Its flesh, pale and chalky, like a giant skull simply left in the soil being subsumed over time by gravity and the ever changing tendrils of thousands of ill fated photosynthetic life forms, grabbing ahold in spring and dying in the fall, leaving a mounting layer of decayed plant limbs across it.

It must have spent those long and solitary months muttering to itself in whatever incomprehensible psychic language is employed by turnips, ruminating on its own loneliness until the sorrow turned to insanity and provided a strange relief from the former, no longer mentally able to process its own sad plight. Abandoned to live among the remains of its own dead compatriots of various species, every blemished mark upon its flesh a potential spawning point for life forms both able and willing to consume its corpulence completely, to leave behind only a small ball of slimy remains.

THE BOOK OF STYXHEXENHAMMER

When plucked from the soil, indeed the turnip, as far as its size, was fine, and the smell of slightly spicy turnip-ness heavy about it, just the way a turnip ought to be, but its void-like face, folded into its own flesh at several points, was a stark reminder of its short and miserable life, which much have been little more than that experienced by the sole remainder of some long-dead tribe clinging to the relevancy of his own ancestors, which he knows will be forgotten completely once he is dead. Its entire reality shattered, turnip-thulhu must have shivered in the cool nights and were it not for the mercy of a hose, would have withered all day in the hot sun, lamenting its own pitiful existence.

There are still no less than three others of its brethren, planted some distance apart in order for their suffering to improve their flavor and scent, all out there ready to be killed and eaten. I wonder, can they feel pain, and when ripped from their discomforted beds of warm soil will they, too, be malformed as though subjected to the Mark of Cain?

The turnip though was quite tasty. I chopped it into pieces, and it ended up cooked until somewhat soft, then mixed with steak juice until fully ready to eat.

X: THE WACK-ASS STORY OF HOW I BECAME MAGICAL

Once upon a time there was a strange hole in my backyard and so like any sane person who was totally not wasted on alcohol I decided to crawl inside and see what I could see. The opening itself was barely large enough to hunch through- perhaps three feet in height, and moist, mossy, slippery to the touch- obviously more or less earthen interspersed with some sedimentary rock, at least for the fist twenty or so feet, angling downward into the earth and finally giving way to merely humidified rock of one sort or another.

This stone path continued for some twenty yards or perhaps slightly less, at a slope not steep enough to be particularly dangerous, but just enough to be glad it wasn't as slick as the overhang above it. As the tunnel leveled back out it also opened up into a more cavernous size, enough to nearly be able to stand- six feet, roughly, just slightly too short for someone a few inches beyond that in height.

This room- for it was obviously carved- was quite odd indeed, and must have been plowed into the rock centuries prior. I examined the walls and found no notable marks, although ridges on their humid surface betrayed them to have been dug at by picks of some kind. The floor was a different story- mostly it was comprised of nothing more than the same generically carved natural stone as the walls were, but in the center of the room was a circle, apparently where one large circular stone intersected its surroundings, looking for all the world like a primitive sewer lid. It was perhaps a yard across, and naturally I began to pry at it with the knife I carried everywhere. The lid at first didn't budge but soon gave way and was surprisingly light, having been at first difficult to move not due to weight (for the stone was thin if strong and not apparently very dense- perhaps a porous mineral of some kind different from the surrounding rock altogether) but because it had been stuck in place by centuries of decayed stone grime, bits of detritus of a decayed nature, of indeterminate source, perhaps the deposits of the lid simply becoming dirt over time by the slow erosion of humidity.

Briefly considering going back up out of the tunnel for a flashlight, I reconsidered as I gazed into what was now a yard-wide hole before me, seeing that at odd points downward there on a seemingly endless vertical shaft were points of light that seemed phosphorescent, emanating from the stone walls themselves- there was a ladder there that looked safe enough, at least by the standards applicable to mysterious, centuries-old ruins of unknown manufacture. The ladder itself was merely metal, possibly corroded bronze- at points it looked like it had been lined on the rungs with wood, and a few bits here and there still bore carvings of some kind, though discolored- whirls and geometric shapes of random character, but these rungs had long ago been worn away mostly and now only stubs grasped tightly to the sides near where each rung was held by the sides of the ladder itself.

I made my way down, feeling with my feet to test each rung, mindful that any particular spot might contain no rung at all and merely a gap, leading to a dangerous situation. After thirty or so feet of descent I came to the first spot of light visible from above to find it was not a phosphorescence of any kind but rather a small cluster of crystals, glowing minutely in that same spot, recessed slightly into the wall. Around the cluster, which sat in a small glass orb, irregular and not very skillfully carved, were little bits of stone that had been carved into bricks, or perhaps a brickwork pattern merely carved into the little crevice. This alcove of light was replicated by others down below, every five or so feet, irregularly lining every side of the shaft save for the one with the latter bolted to it.

Soon my foot met with floor and not rung. At first it looked like the shaft was a dead end leading nowhere, but on suspicion there was more to see I grabbed one chunk of the crystal glowing above my head and held it before me like a weak torch, feeling and looking at the wall. There was, indeed, as suspected, a thin line in roughly a rectangular shape opposite the ladder, and a fairly slight push was all that was needed to send it back, swinging around to reveal another tunnel- this one high enough to stand in fully, although freakishly narrow- narrow enough to prevent passage by anyone with claustrophobia. The stone door creaked and groaned like a millstone slowly grinding flour for the first time in a few centuries of disuse but stayed back when put there. To prevent the possibility that a gust of air might somehow shut it behind me I kicked several bits of wooden coating off the lowest rungs of the ladder and shoved them under the door where a small uneven patch in the tunnel permitted it to be done, then hesitated and set the glowing crystal torch down, ascending the ladder to the second glowing chunk of the same, plucking it loose so as to have two of them- that way, if one was damaged, somehow, I wouldn't be sitting there impotently in darkness trying to feel my way back out.

The feeling of stagnation was heavy in this further tunnel which thankfully was not all that long. It yawned outward into a gigantic cathedral-like arrangement, perhaps a hundred feet tall but relatively thin, a room with a silvery floor and a line of pillars built into the walls themselves- the stone here was of a lighter color than prior, a sort of off-gray with shimmering green inclusions like some sort of mica-infused rock. Haphazardly around the walls, which were roughly hewn and therefore not entirely even, were bits of the shining crystals from before, but here apparently natively grown and not covered by glass or

30

placed for light, but had no doubt been there when the room was mined out in the first place.

Some twenty yards or so ahead was a small lectern and I made my way to it, careful not to step on any potential traps or loose spots which might send me very likely cascading into a bottomless pit, into some ultimate darkness- the lectern was no simple affair and could have passed for a fairly modern art nouveau piece if the rest of the chambers didn't belie a likely antiquated origin, what with the use of bronze rather than, say, wrought iron or some more modern steel or alloy. Its bottom was carved with patterns which resembled flowing feet, cascading down along the four corners (which were in turn rounded off somewhat) which were further carved with branching fern leaves- each leaf was intricate, upon further study even including proper veins. Above this, rising from the fern-feet was the stand itself which was more simple on the surface (which of course was flat, having only a slightly stylized ridge at its bottom to hold a book to be placed there) but all around the sides of the thing were wonderful pictures which seemed to have been etched by heat or flame, not by a chisel- browned in form and apparently coated with some sort of agent to give them a shine- a sort of antiquated lacquer. The figures were those of the twelve zodiacal signs- three on each side.

I heard a soft sound just then as I held and studied the lectern- it seemed to be coming, muffled, from behind the wall immediately to the right of the lectern some ten feet distant. I stopped and held my breath, now aware even of the movement of blood through my veins due to the immense stillness of the stone hall, and again heard it, a little louder due to my own silence- indeed, a sound like chuckling, as though someone was enjoying the spectacle of me wondering over their lectern, watching me somehow through a wall of solid rock.

THE BOOK OF STYXHEXENHAMMER

Making my way down from the lectern space to the stone wall I held an ear to it. Definitively, once more, was the sound- not a chuckling perhaps, it was hard to tell- it certainly sounded like it, but may have been a sob, or perhaps someone mumbling in their sleep. Since the hall was lit by so many crystals it wasn't difficult to search the wall for an opening and I found it- a door-shaped line which I figured on pushing open- but it did not budge. Scratching my head, I quickly owed myself a fool and stuck my pocket knife into the crack, which was no small feat for the door fit its doorway almost to perfection; prying at it produced a result quickly, as though the door was oiled and well maintained- it didn't even creak but fell away towards me. I held my knife in one hand and raised one of the glowing crystal clusters before my face to peer inside, and was immediately blasted by a gust of wind that sent me careening backwards into the lectern, which after all was not bolted down and simply toppled on its side, flipping several times and ending up against the opposite wall.

The wall before me, as I staggered to my knees and patted myself down, worried I might well have fallen on my knife and stabbed myself (thankfully that wasn't the case) began to fall away entirely- all the way up nearly to the rounded ceiling. Chunks of rock exploded in all directions and before me stood a gigantic demon- it had to be forty feet tall, and instead of a forehead it had a giant ass. It turned and I could see then that its actual face was below its tail where its ass should be, as though the unfortunate creature had been mistreated by some wizard centuries ago who decided to give it a most cruel and sadistic fate.

Just then the thing smashed one fist into its own head and grabbed a piece of rock with the other, gnawing it and looking for a moment like it didn't even know I was there, but then it roared and I decided it was high time to flee. The demon grabbed the side of the wall and vaulted itself around like an orangutan swinging around a palm tree, breaking a section of pillar off as it did. I could hear it moan in pain as it rammed the jagged rock into its own stomach, and from its face-ass I heard it shout "TRUMP WILL WIN THE NEXT ELECTION!"

It roared again and shoved both hands in its stomach wound, pulling it open. A massive jet of hot demon blood shot out and slammed me right in the face as I continued to try and flee to the next hall. The sizzling pain caused me to collapse and my last memory there was of the demon doing cartwheels and laughing maniacally twenty feet behind my body.

When I came to I was on the ground in the forest not ten yards from my own home. Next to me was a little pouch. I opened it and it contained a thank you note signed "The demon that just trolled you" and a little piece of what appeared to be demonic candy that said "eat me." I did, felt enlightened, and since that day have been able to make political predictions and grow very large collard plants.

CONCLUSION

I hope you enjoyed reading this swill s much as I enjoyed writing it. Especially the part about getting hit in the face with a jet of demon blood, or how you can make tasty things out of dead spiders.

Indeed this work is truly a psycho-social statement regarding the finer aspects of the baroque period with all of its glory and grandeur, the flowing curves and radiance of such grand depictions as those of Caravaggio or Rubens. Behold the spectacular glow of the hair, the religious iconography, and all such piffle and balderdash. Truly a gift of god that we may witness such divine spectacles writ large on canvas before us preserved for such long ages.

Actually scratch that, I'm just weird.

Made in the USA
Middletown, DE
18 August 2019